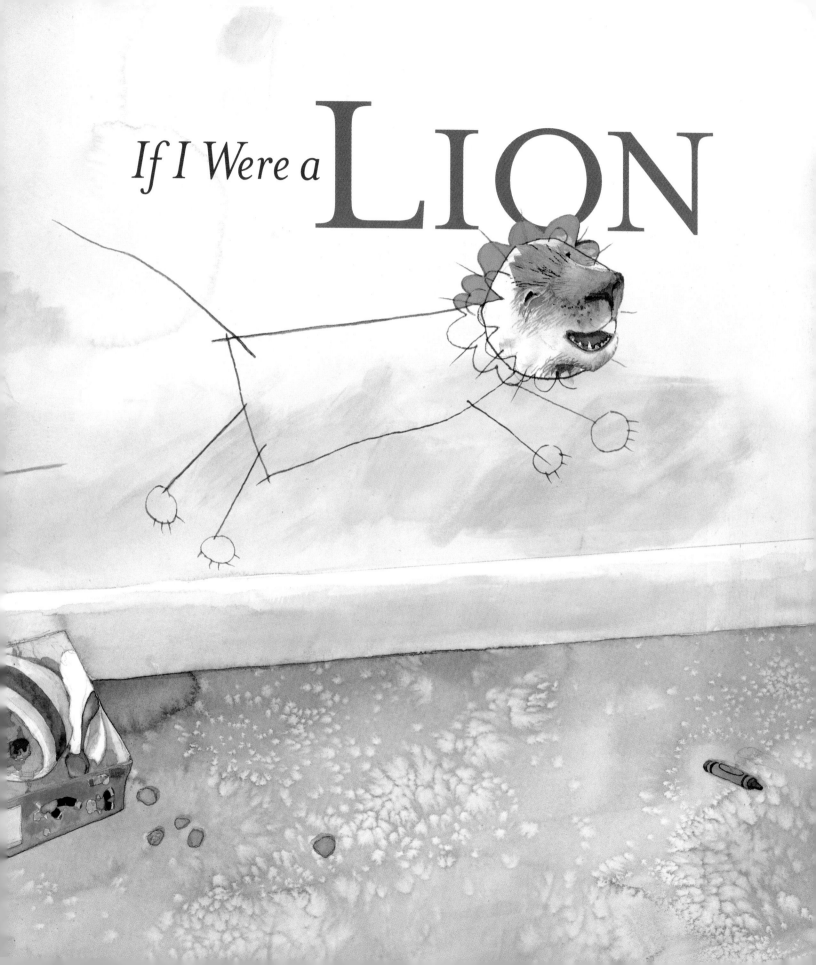

If I Were a LION

For my Whistlepig pals, Tom and Dan
—S. W.
For Rennie, Hannah, and Zoë
—H. M. S.

Aladdin Paperbacks
An imprint of Simon & Schuster Children's Publishing Division
1230 Avenue of the Americas, New York, NY 10020
Text copyright © 2004 by Sarah Weeks
Illustrations copyright © 2004 by Heather M. Solomon
Also available in an Atheneum Books for Young Readers hardcover edition.
Designed by Polly Kanevsky
The text of this book was set in Carlton.
The illustrations for this book were rendered in watercolor and gouache.
Manufactured in China
First Aladdin Paperbacks edition July 2007
12 14 16 18 20 19 17 15 13 11
The Library of Congress has cataloged the hardcover edition as follows:
Weeks, Sarah.
If I were a lion / Sarah Weeks ; illustrated by Heather M. Solomon.—1st ed.
p. cm.
Summary: A young girl imagines how wild she could be if she were an animal.
[1. Behavior—Fiction. 2. Imagination—Fiction. 3. Animals—Fiction. 4. Stories in rhyme.]
I. Solomon, Heather M. ill. II. Title.
PZ8.3.W4125 If 2004
[E]—dc21 2002011459
ISBN-13: 978-0-689-84836-0 (hc.)
ISBN-13: 978-1-4169-3837-8 (pbk.)
0915 SCP

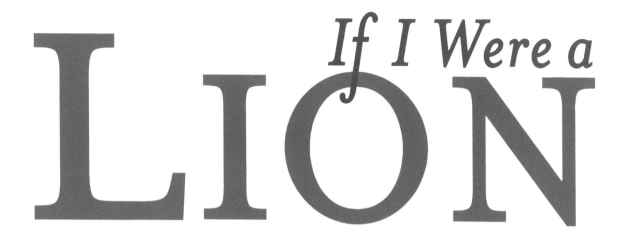

If I Were a LION

Written by **Sarah Weeks**

Illustrated by *Heather M. Solomon*

ALADDIN PAPERBACKS

NEW YORK LONDON TORONTO SYDNEY

I'm sitting in the time-out chair
because my mother
put me there.
She said,
"You try my
patience, child!
I do not like it
when you're
wild."

Wild?

Who me?

That's so absurd.

How could she even use that word?

If I were a lion,
I'd growl and roar
and knock the dishes
on the floor.
I'd scare the hair
right off the cat,
but do you see me
doing that?

If I were a bear,
I'd have big claws.
I'd rip up pillows with my paws.
I'd scratch and poke
and pierce and tear,
not sit here nicely in my chair.

Am I howling?
Do I bark?
Rummage through
the trash at dark?

Greet my visitors like this?

No. Not me. I hug and kiss.

Do I snarl?
Do I snap?
Climb a tree to take a nap?
Look at me;
I'm meek and mild,
about a million miles
from wild.

Wild is woolly.

Wild is wet.

Wild's as naughty as you get.

Wild's ferocious.

Wild will bite.

I'm precocious
and polite.

Wild has feathers.

Wild has scales.

Wild has whiskers, tusks, and tails.

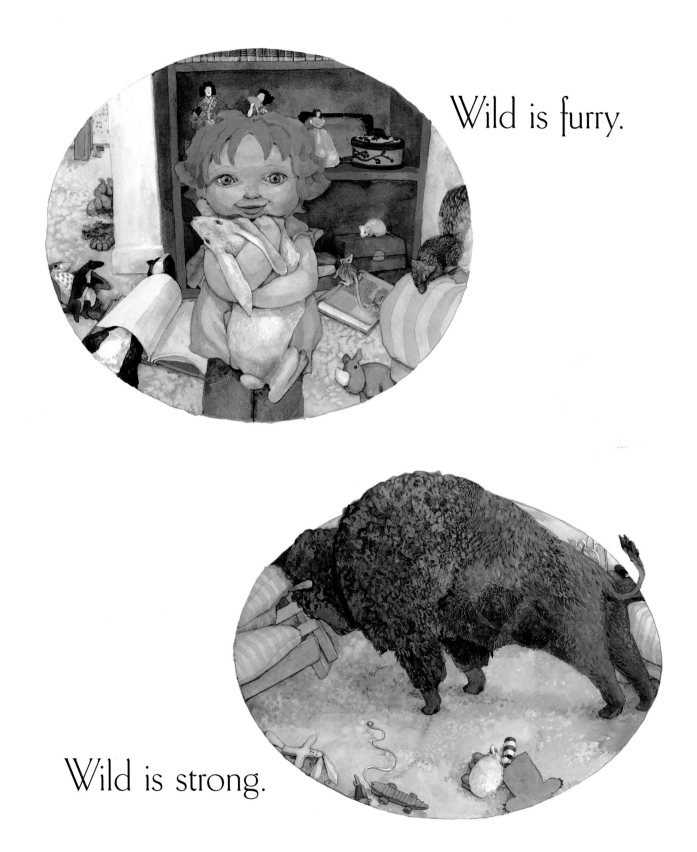

Wild is furry.

Wild is strong.

Wild does not know
right from wrong.

Mother doesn't realize
that lions don't apologize.

But when she does,
then she will see,
the opposite of wild is . . .

. . . me.